I LUST YOU

CHE ARUNACHALAM

To all the beautiful women in my life...

Contents

Foreword — vii

Preface — ix

Acknowledgements — xi

Prologue — xiii

1. Chapter 1 — 1

2. Chapter 2 — 12

3. Chapter 3 — 16

4. Chapter 4 — 23

5. Chapter 5 — 27

6. Chapter 6 — 32

7. Chapter 7 — 35

8. Chapter 8 — 36

Foreword

The journey of lust to love.

Preface

Started as a small awareness writeup speaking about the importance of female sexual satisfaction and orgasm which turned out to be a story from all the inspirations I faced with lust and love. This book also stands as a closure for people I have never had a closure with. I am dedicated to all those beautiful women who came across my journey and made me a better person. This is also an expression of guilt. As I mentioned in this novel "Rehabilitated hearts always deserve a chance".

Acknowledgements

Gratitude
To everyone who stood with me and helped me to bring
my dream of releasing my first novel.
Thanking all the women who came across my life.

Prologue

It's not Love versus Lust, It's always Love and Lust.

CHAPTER I

A desperate body is more beautiful than a hopeless heart. Yeah, we women are better actors when it comes to sex. Seems like you people are shocked to hear this. Okay, let's do a practical test here. So here there are nearly 300 women, how many of you had satisfied sex? Just raise your hands. Come on, don't hesitate, if you had hesitated you wouldn't have come here to attend this seminar right? Okay, let me ask this way how many of you haven't had satisfying sex ever in your whole life? After a few seconds of silence, I saw an aunt raising her hand. Starting from her, almost everyone raised their hands.

Now Listen, Reportedly 80% of Indian women are not satisfied with their sexual life. Many women do not orgasm during sex. The main reason behind this is their partner doesn't pay much attention to clitoral stimulations or the other things that drive us to the bed. The importance of sexual satisfaction is an important topic to discuss because it is associated with higher levels of love and stability in one's relationship. Nearly 25% to 60% of women suffer from some form of sexual dysfunction, which means having low interest in sex because of the difficulties in achieving orgasm. Here, especially in India sex is all about penetrating the penis inside the vulva. Eighty percent of women need clitoral stimulation to have better orgasms, penetrative sex alone doesn't do the job. Let's prioritize our sexual needs from today. Thank You. I finished my seminar and came down the dais. I heard someone calling my name from behind.

Mandhakini. An old lady lady aged around 60 called me.

I'm Jency, it was nice to hear you. Can I ask you something? She asked.

Sure Amma.

Are you married?

No Amma.

Then how can you speak so many things relatable to all the married women here?

Because marriage isn't alone, not the way to experience dissatisfied sex right? I said and she laughed. After getting out I was heading towards my friend's hen party. As usual, I'm the late bee in our gang. Once I parked my car I found a stranger at the corner of the parking lot struggling to light up his cigarette with his empty lighter. I thought I would help him with mine but hesitated and moved to the lift.

Excuse me. I heard a voice.

You're Miss Mandhakini, right? The cigarette guy asked me.

Yes.

Then you must have a lighter, can you please pass it on?

Excuse me? I asked.

Yeah please, I'm just struggling with this lighter for nearly 15 mins.

Well... okay but how do you know me and how do you know that I smoke?

Because I do follow you on your social media accounts and by the way, it was nice to meet you.

Seriously?

Well yeah maybe. He said.

Okay, do you have another cigarette?

Nah.. maybe we can share it? He asked.

Yeah okay. I said and went towards him. He was fully bald with a well-trimmed beard and wearing a dark green shirt and faded yellow pants. Neatly tucked and with a pair of brown shoes. Surprised to see someone who matched the colors of his belt and shoes, wait also his shirt and his socks. I went near him and flamed the lighter for him. After 3 puffs, he handed over the cigarette to me.

Who are you by the way? I asked.

I'm... just a common man of this republic.

Well, do you have a name?

Yes, I do. He said and asked for his turn to smoke.

Then say it nah?

Oh yeah. I'm Che.

Don't pay the fool, I'm asking for your real name. I said. He gave the cigarette to me and took his wallet to show his ID proof and I continued to smoke the rest. He showed his license.

Did you change it or that's your name itself? I asked.

So you'll believe me only if I show my birth certificate right?

No, Che isn't a common name here in India, right? So... yeah.

Dad loves Che Guevara.

Oh cool, and you're?

An entrepreneur.

Okay. I said and I was about to throw away the cigarette and he stopped me.

Wait, give it to me. It comes around 2 to 3 puffs and you gonna waste it just like that? He said and got the cigarette from my hand. Then I decided to go to the hen party and start moving after saying thanks for the cigarette.

So what's your plan? He asked when I was walking towards the lift.

Does that have anything to do with you? I asked.

It might.

No, it can't. I said and started heading towards the lift and pressed the lift button. I turned towards him and he was stamping the cigarette under his foot. Before he looked at me I thought of asking what's his plan for the day.

So What's your plan? I shouted from the lift to that corner where he was.

Well, I'm just heading to meet a few people now and I'm planning to leave the hotel by 11. He said. I just didn't say anything and by the time the lift came. It was already 8 PM and I was too lethargic for the bachelorette party. Once I got to the rooftop I saw my bunch of girls who had already started the party and I was the only one who was dressed in formals with a blazer on me. I approached them, greeted everyone with a hug, and started searching for the bride.

Where's Shruthi? I asked them.

She's in the restroom with Dharshi. Said Jenny.

Huh?

I mean she wanted to try tequila today but as usual, she started puking it.

See you guys know that her appetites are not fit enough then why are you people encouraging it?

Miss Lecturer, please stop lecturing and here have a sip. Said Madhu, who gave me a tequila shot. Later Shruthi joins us and she's already not in the right state to enjoy the party but the girls keep celebrating until it's 11. From nowhere I remembered Che saying that he would be leaving by 11. I called Dharshi and asked her to take care of Shruthi and stood up and started walking towards the lift. Once the lift opened, yeah it was him with a few other people. He just nodded his head with a smile and passed me. Just after a few seconds, I heard him calling me from behind.

Mandhakini? I was so cautious that I was not expecting to meet him and turned towards him.

Well, you forgot your lighter. He said and passed it to me.

Thank you. I said and we had a moment of silence together. Suddenly I heard Dharshi calling me. I interrupted the silence and ran towards her and saw Shruthi puking again. I took her to the washroom and while passing through I saw him watching me from a corner. Once I was back he was at the edge of the rooftop and smoking. Without hesitation, I went towards him.

Can I join you? I asked and he silently passed on the cigarette that he was smoking.

It must be an unforgettable hen party for her right? He said and smiled a bit.

Actually for all of us.

Maybe yeah.

So you didn't leave?

Should I? He asked and I was left in silence and a pinch of smile over my face. I guessed he had found out that I kinda like him.

You're right. He said and I was shocked for a second.

Sorry?

I mean your seminar on the importance of female sexual satisfaction.

You were there?

I watched it on your Instagram Live.

Oh, so you agree with what I said?

Many forms of sexual expression can help to improve sexual life, it would have been great if you had talked about it too.

So can you share what are those? I asked.

Are you testing me?

No, if you're wrong I might correct it, right? I said and looked at him and passed the cigarette.

Make sense.

Go ahead.

I feel that Oral sex stands first when comes to satisfying female orgasm. He said looking at the sky. It seemed like he was trying to ignore my looks.

Okay?

Oral sex means sharing orgasm. Oral sex can be a natural and pleasurable part of sex between partners if both of them enjoy it with consent to it.

Continue. I said looking at him.

It's the sexiest thing one can do with their partner. He said and turned towards me and that second I turned on his right and acted as if I wasn't looking at him.

Any comments? He asked.

Finish your stand.

To have healthy oral sex, get your partner's consent before you start, and make frequent eye contact since it will make the moment good. Using our hands and breath to make them feel the actual pleasure. Use both tongue and lips, maybe you might feel it eerie especially for beginners but there's nothing wrong with feeling so, right? Gently start to use your mouth on your partner's vulva/vagina or penis. If one is looking to explore more oral sex, then drive with all parts of their mouth. And finally being hygiene, yeah in oral sex one should make sure that they are hygienic. So yeah, sex is not only about intercourse. He said and both were looking at each other for a moment.

Impressed. I said and heard Jenny calling me from behind.

Excuse me. I said and went towards the girl's gang. They were about to leave and asked me to take the car. I looked at them and gave my car key to Jenny since she was the only person who wasn't drunk. I told her to drop everyone home and would get my car tomorrow. I saw him waiting for me.

So it was nice meeting you. See you. He said.

Are you for real? I asked and he laughed a bit and said that he noticed giving my car key to my friend.

So what I was saying? I asked.

That you got impressed. He said and I had a smile on my face which can't be shown.

So where do you learn this all?

I don't know. He said and looked at me.

Anyhow I do agree with whatever you said but.

But?

Knowledge is different from personal experience.

So?

So, by the way, what's your plan now? I asked him.

To drop you home.

You're just too good with words.

Maybe I'm.

Shall we? He asked.

Where?

Huh! For a walk? He said.

We both came down to the streets and we looked on both sides and thought about where to start. Wait, is it normal to go for a walk with a stranger? That too at midnight? Okay, Mandhakini, don't overthink, just be in the moment.

So where are we heading to? I asked.

Towards Pondy Bazaar.

Why? Because we reach Panangal Park right?

Yeah so? I asked.

From there it's easy to get to your home so yeah?

Wait, have you been stalking me? Oh my god, now I'm scared. I said and looked at him.

See it's you who told your friend that your house is near Panangal Park so that you'll walk from here and hand over your car key.

You overhear it? I asked.

Shall we? He asked.

Yeah. As we started walking we started sharing many things about ourselves from where we studied and what made him follow my social media profiles and too many interesting conversations and at one point we wantedly took the longest route to my home.

So why are you so interesting? I asked him and he turned towards me.

No, I'm not. I'm just being honest.

Okay, that's a nice one. Any past relationships?

Excuse me, why can't you ask me "Are you in a relationship?" Do I look like a single guy? He asked me.

See, in the past hour you didn't text anyone, you received 4 calls and that too business calls so it's obvious that you're single.

Your assumption is absolutely..... By the time he completes the sentence, I pray that my assumption will be right. Okay yeah, I like him.

Right. He said and looked at me. I was trying hard to hide the satisfied feeling on my face.

Why aren't you asking me if I'm in a relationship or not?

Because I know you're not.

How? I asked.

I know.

What if I say I'm in a relationship?

If you say so then it's easy for me to find that it's a lie.

Oh!

Yeah.

Hey... don't play with words okay? I said.

I'm not. He said and we came near to my house.

Join me for a drink?

Come let's go.

Hey hey....

What? Now don't say it's just a formality invite. I know it's not just for formality.

Okay Comrade Che, get in. We moved upstairs and he made himself comfortable and I went in to take two glasses and half a bottle of Old Monk. By the time I changed my outfit and wore a loose tee, and comfortable shorts. He was looking at my book collection and I was watching him from behind to check what book he chose. He took Ian Kerner's "She Comes First" from the left corner of the shelf and turned towards me. She started noticing me from top to bottom and I started looking at the floor and was waiting for him to talk.

Do I have anything to change? He asked.

Is it okay if it's from a female closet? Do you mind?

I don't. He said.

Come in. I said and he kept the book on the table and followed me.

Here's a tee, obviously it's oversized so it will fit you but my shorts won't fit you. What else do I have? I kept on searching my closet and looked at him.

Are you fine with my skirt? I said and gave a mischievous look but I wasn't ready to hear okay from him. Yes, he said okay and I gave him the skirt and left the room. He changed and came back to my room. What am I doing? I have got a stranger in my room wearing my skirt like a lungi. He was looking around my room and there was a bit of silence around us. He said that he was obsessed with the golden color lighting in my room and took the book back from the table.

So what's it about?

It's a book for men to relearn how can they pleasure their partners and how to actively listen when women share their sexual preferences.

Go ahead.

Go ahead, what? I asked.

Your sexual preferences.

Is there any intention behind knowing my sexual preferences? I asked him.

I don't know.

Okay, yeah okay. I said to him and two glass pegs of an old monk. I was sitting on my ground-level bed and he was sitting opposite to me in my bean bag. Randomly I started noticing whether his nails were cut or not. Now I don't know what's my intention behind it. We shared cheers and suddenly my phone rang. It was Dharshi. She called me to check if I was home. That ringtone made me scared as the silence prevailed between us. He was waiting for me to start.

Have you heard of A-Spot? I asked him.

Sorry, the G-spot?

No, the A-spot, not many people are familiar with the A-spot and the amount of pleasure it can bring. It's present on the lower side of your vaginal opening. The region is filled with nerve endings. So that's my top sexual preference when it comes to oral sex.

Interesting. Then?

Clitoris.

Expected.

See, It's common knowledge that the clitoris is one of the most sensitive spots on a woman's body. It has 8,000 nerve endings that ultimately make it the powerhouse of pleasure. But that's not it. These nerve endings further spread the sensation to 15,000 other pelvis nerves, which is why clitoral orgasms are truly an OMG feeling.

Then?

Mastering clitoral stimulation takes some practice. Although fingers do the job the best, you can also introduce some tongue action. I said and I was looking at him. He was looking at the book and looked at me.

So now I need to read this book to relearn how men can give pleasure to their partners.

Practical knowledge is more helpful than theoretical knowledge.

CHAPTER II

Sorry? He said.

You know what I meant. I said and he was hiding a smile by looking at his glass and looking at me.

According to you, What does sex mean? I asked him.

Sex is something that is not alone about naked bodies, it gets its meaning only when our emotions are naked along with our body.

Agreed. Ever had such a moment in the past? Like being emotionally naked with someone.

I'm too unlucky when it comes to emotional nudity. He said and smiled. That smile wasn't a good one.

Why do you say that?

People prioritize naked bodies over naked emotions. He said and looked at me. I asked him to come and sit on my bed. He stood up and came forward and sat near me and leaned on the wall.

Been years. I said.

What?

I mean to share the bed with someone. I said.

Like, How many days?

3 years.

Oh, so do you regret this moment?

No, I'm not. I said and there was a silence prevailed for some moment. We refilled our glasses and both were leaning on the wall and, slowly we started holding hands.

I was in an abusive relationship for 4 years. I said and he turned towards me.

Yeah, it was abusive to the core and you're the first person I'm sharing. Things were fine for the first few months, but.... No, I don't wanna talk about it. I'm sorry. I said and tried to hide my tears from him. By the time he tightly held my hand, said it was okay, and tried to empathize with me.

I'm a victim of a false sexual accusation. Yeah, it was 3 years back and from then I started keeping myself away from all the women in my life. Including my mom. He said and looked at me with a smile.

Then? I asked.

Truth needs its own time but until then the sufferings will be alone.

How were you managing things until that?

I wasn't. I feel this is my second life.

I'm so sorry, I shouldn't have brought this. I said and tried to lean on his shoulder.

If you didn't, we wouldn't have initiated the nudity of emotions within us.

Yeah, can I have your consent? I asked him and looked at him by leaning on his shoulder.

For?

For this. I said and kissed his right cheek, once I kissed him I realized what I'd done and within seconds I went away from him.

I'm sorry. I said and saw our hands were still holding each other and slowly we let them free, both of us were hesitating to look at each other for some time and the moment we both looked at each other we started sharing our lips. Yeah, we did. Yes, we kissed each other. Slowly we saw each other by holding our cheeks and I don't know if it's coincidence or what, we both had our eyes wet when we were looking at each other. We both took away our hands and turned towards the opposite wall before the bed. It was already 4 in the morning, but like all fantasy filmy songs I wished, I manifested that this night shouldn't end.

Wish nothing could stop this moment. He said and held my hands. I turned to him.

What? You too thought the same? I asked.

Yeah.

Can the sunrise stop us from what we have now?

Definitely not. I said and pulled his tee and dragged him towards me. He was literally on me and we had nil gap between us and had a small gap between our lips. That's the last gap between our lips until we decide to go further and explore the intimacy we have. His lips slowly started traveling straight down from my lips to my neck. I wasn't ready for those love bites but his consent before getting there made me feel important and I received them with love.

Do you mind if I?

If you? I asked.

If I help you to remove your tee?

Oh, when did I say that I want to remove them? I said and gave a mischievous look.

You have all the consent, Che. I said and then he kept one hand on my waist and another on the back side of my tee. He slowly evolved his hand into my tee and the sense of his hand on my waist made me go crazy and I pulled away his tee before he could pull off. Maybe I was furious but he wanted to win me slowly and steadily. Did I say he wants to win me? He already did. He pulled off my tee and that's the moment I started feeling the pain in my ears. Yeah, the tee got stuck between my earrings and my hair. I literally shouted and he made me calm and gently removed them and my earrings spoiled the moment. He was concentrating on my ears without realizing that I was lying before him with a bra. I said it was fine and he kissed my forehead and said that he was sorry.

By the way, I love your breasts. He said.

You haven't witnessed them fully.

Do you mind?

Che, here's your last warning. If you are going to ask consent for each and everything then...

Then? He asked.

Hey, don't try to be smart here, no word games. I said and we were sharing laughter and that's the moment I realized that this is what I was missing for years together. Those few drops of tears, sharing happiness, sharing our deepest darkness, our insecurities, and of course the true us. All these things happened that night. He made me understand that emotional satisfaction is as important as sexual satisfaction in bed. I was unlucky when it came to clitoris simulation until he went down on me. To be honest, he was the first person to get down on me without any hesitation and gave importance to my satisfaction. We didn't have penetrative sex that night but we were satisfied with heaven. We were cuddling each other and I turned towards him. Looked at him and asked....

Do you wanna say something?

Yes. He said.

Go ahead.

I L... I kept my hand over his mouth and said...

I Lust You.

CHAPTER III

So, you slept with a stranger? Asked Madhu.

What the fuck? Stop calling him a stranger. I said.

Excuse me, Miss Mandhakini, so what is he?

A new friend, Maybe.

Just friend? She asked.

Yeah.

Okay, tell me something, I know you are a demisexual so how come this happened?

Madhu, why are you enquiring me this much?

Because you have done something that you usually don't do, she said and looked at me.

See, Yes, I'm a demisexual, Yes, I don't go just like that and sleep with a stranger, yes, I've done something which usually I won't do, But I don't know, with him I had this feeling of that my kind of thing with him and it just happened.

Okay, so what's next?

I don't know Madhu, I wish he would feel the same way I felt. I said, and I looked at her with a pitiful face.

But, what if he didn't?

Fuck You.

What? There are possibilities, right? She asked me.

Yeah, but I don't feel so.

Okay, Call him.

What? I asked.

What? Just call him nah?

I don't have his number.

What? Are you guys even serious? Now it sounds like a one-night stand for me.

No, it's not. We were just in the moment and he left.

Didn't he say anything before he leaves?

Yeah, he came near me and kissed me and said "Until next time" and left.

Okay? Do you know any of his social media handles?

No, But I know that he follows me. I said.

Okay, come let's search.

Okay, I gave her an innocent kid's accent and she stared at me.

What's his name? She asked.

Che.

Huh?

Che. I stressed it.

Just Che?

Yeah. I said and she started searching for him in my Facebook followers but she didn't have any luck, later she moved to Instagram and continued searching for him. Then we found his profile and there was no doubts about the profile because it was a public account which is overfilled with his pictures. Madhu opened the DM and texted him "Hi" and we started to wait for a reply from his side and by that time we decided to stalk his Instagram profile.

After a while, we received a text from him.

"See you tomorrow at The Beer Barrels by 7 PM"

Isn't too fast? Madhu asked me and I was looking confused but at the same time, I knew I gonna make it. Later after Madhu left, I tried to text him back but ended up disappointed since I didn't receive any reply from his side. I had many thoughts and questions in me starting with "Is he showing off?" to "Is he really busy? Or does he just want to make me wait?" with all these disempowering thoughts

I fell asleep and suddenly I woke up in the middle of the night for a pee. I went to the loo and came back to bed and felt the notification vibration from my phone. Yes, it was him.

Still up? He texted.

Yeah, seems like you were busy.

Yeah, Just finished work and came to bed.

So, is it common to work this late?

Sometimes, yeah.

So then. I texted him.

Then.... Are we meeting tomorrow?

Maybe. I said.

Maybe?

Yeah, I do have work, right? That too by evening, I guess it's not possible. I said.

Okay.

Okay. I said and he saw my text and I didn't receive any reply from him.

Okay, I'll be there by 7, so if you're free, let's meet.

Yeah, will let you know. I said.

Good night then.

Yeah, Good Night. I said and I started blushing by looking at our chat and moved to sleep. I hardly tried not to disclose to him how desperate I was to meet him since he left my place. But at the same time, I know that he would easily find it the moment he sees me in person. All I need to do is to maintain a posture tomorrow when I meet him.

SATURDAY
15:02 HRS

"Phone Notification"

"Hey, if you are coming today, let me know"

Wait, should I tell him or should I plan a surprise visit? Wait, No, what if he didn't turn up if I say I'm not coming?

Fuck, Why am I overthinking this much and sounds like a teenage kid who's new to these kinds of feelings. After all this overthinking, I replied to him "Okay".

Time was flying away and I was sitting and looking at my attire and dealing with my insecurities about wearing it. Yes, it was a Backless Red Shoulder Strap Bodycon dress. I just bought it a few months back to embrace my semi-pear-shaped body but the confidence I had when I bought it didn't last long. Embracing my body is the biggest untold battle I face whenever I open my closet. I always feel I am not proportional when I see the second half of my body. After an hour of self-talk, I finally decided to wear the Bodycon for the first time. I tied a large portion of my hair and left a few as curls to look good for this backless outfit. After wearing it, for the first time, I adored my butt from the side, although I hated it all my life. Self-obsession took so much time that I was almost getting late to meet him. Later I booked a cab to the ECR and reached there by 18:01, yeah, my excitement in meeting him brought me an hour early but I shouldn't have gotten in this early and proved to him how desperate I was to meet him. I went in and I noticed each and everyone's eyes were on me. I moved straight to the bar counter and took a seat I was looking around for him, but he was nowhere and then I turned to the bartender.

Mam, here's your neat glass of Old Monk, Sir will be here in a few minutes. Said the bartender.

Excuse me? I said and he replied to me with a smile and turned to the next customer. I was left confused and took my phone to text him. I texted him to know if he was already here but left with no reply. I had a visit of the Restobar with a glass of rum in my hand and I loved the vintage theme they gave. Suddenly the bartender came towards me.

Mam, can I guide you to Sir?

Sorry?

I mean, Sir asked me to take you to his office.

Sure. I followed him and opened the door to his office, I saw him coming towards me in a neat white shirt tucked in with navy blue pants and made me sit in. In this confusion, I forgot to notice his reaction to my outfit, all I noticed was he was stuck at the place where he was when I entered his office.

Hello, Che.

Such a cruel bitch you are. He said.

Sorry?

Can't you see me, like you made me breathless and...

And?

Look at you, your outfit hugs the curves of your body and makes me jealous.

Jealous? Why?

My job is being stolen by your outfit. I thought I embraced your curves more than this outfit.

Too smooth, tell me where did you learn this?

Learn what?

To grab one's attention and curiosity through words.

Well, you own half of the credits too.

See. Again. I said and he came forward to hug me, he placed his hand on the back of my shoulders. I felt the warmth in his hands and I put my head on his shoulder and kissed there without even thinking he was in a white shirt. I placed my lipstick stain over there and looked at him. He slowly took his hand to my waist, there was no disturbance until the DJ started playing jazz on the ground floor.

So? I asked.

Hmm.... Can we go to the terrace?

Yeah, Hey wait, any chance do you own this place?

Yes, I am.

Oh?

Shall we?

Yeah. I said and we reached the terrace and were surprised to see a Skyview bar and lounge.

Isn't this place open for customers?

It is, not for the day.

Why? He just smiled back and made me sit. He sat opposite me and I tried to ignore his looks but he continued seeing me.

Why are you looking at me like this?

I'm just gazing.

Am I worth enough to gaze?

You're worth enough to rule and overrule me. He said and gave his hand and I didn't give my hand back, instead I raised my foot towards his face.

You want to get ruled right?

Yes, my Highness.

Then follow my comments. I said in a husky voice looking into his eyes. He came down to his knees and I kept my foot on his face. I forced my foot towards his face and asked him to bend down.

Che, get down on me.

Yes, my Highness. He said and kept his hand on the dress and pushed it up, within a few seconds, I interrupted him.

Che, Stop, I'm sorry.

Why? What happened? He asked.

I didn't shave. I said and he came towards me and held my neck with one hand, came closer.

I don't mind. He said and he passed his other hand inside my dress through my navel towards my vulva. He touched my clitoris and put pressure over there with his pointing finger. I started feeling the struggle to have a peaceful breath. He passed through the vagina by placing his nails to induce and stimulate me to go crazy. He slowly goes down by placing his lips down on my body to my vulva. He went through it and placed his tongue on my vestibule. I was screaming out of pleasure and he placed his lips and started kissing my vaginal opening. It is a nice place to visit but I don't want his tongue to get stuck there, please go back to the clitoris. I didn't know that my inner voice was louder or what, he just pursued what I thought of. All my insecurities about my lower body flew away the way he owns and celebrates it, the way he kisses my inner thighs and stays there by treating me as His Highness. The silence prevailed after the storm of lust, it felt like the peace I was looking for.

Che.

Yes, He said with slow breathing.

Nothing.

Huh?

CHAPTER IV

I have never thought in my entire life that I would sleep naked under a blanket on a terrace hearing the music of waves from the Bay of Bengal. He was cuddling me from my back and I turned towards him and looked at him. I saw him in his deep sleep, I touched his face, and unfortunately, I woke him up.

You didn't sleep? He asked me in a quavering voice and I was just looking at him.

What? He asked me.

What is Love? I asked him.

Huh? What?

What is Love?

Well..., Love isn't just a feeling. It's an everyday commitment, physically and emotionally.

Then? I asked him.

Then, What?

Tell me more. I said and looked at him.

Love is where we should heal together by creating a safe space for each other to keep growing & evolving together, learning together from love, and growing from love.

Have you thought of being in such a relationship again?

I have but...

But? I asked with a curiosity.

Someday, I want to be committed to someone who has mature plans for our future together. Not just a fling, not just for fun, but a serious relationship.

23

So, what are we? Am I your Fling or whatever we have around us is just fun?

I see you, I see us as the beginning of a beautiful future. He said and looked at me.

How do you say that?

I don't know, it's some kind of feeling I get from you and I feel that even you feel the same. He said. The moment he said that I moved closer and locked my lips with his. I explored his lips with my tongue. Varying the speed until the kiss makes us breathless. Slowly he passed the kiss from my lips to the backside of my neck and slowly came down and kissed my sternum. He gently kneaded my breasts and kissed them equally. He used his mouth to draw very light circles around my nipples gently flicking my areola with his tongue and slowly took my nipple in him. I thought he must forget that I've another breast but how he forgets. He slowly came up and the sun too.

The charms of your body are countless. He said.

Why are you making me blush? I asked him.

Why do I feel like saying something....? He said.

Then, please don't say.

Sure? He asked me.

Yes, Don't say. I said and hid my tears from him.

MONDAY

01:25 HRS

Madhu....Madhu... Get up. I made her wake from sleep and she woke up in the middle of the night by shouting at me but went silent when she noticed me in tears.

Mandhakani? What happened? Asked Madhu.

I love him.

Who?

Che.

Okay, but why are you crying?

I love him but I don't want him to suffer by staying in a relationship with me.

See, Why are you overthinking?

No, I'm not, I don't want him to deal with my struggles, fears, and doubts that made my life horrible after my past relationship. It's like I want him, I can sense that he's already into me but he deserves someone who prioritizes his feelings and emotions instead I would depend on him to join the battles that I go through.

Mandhakini...I agree with you but for how long? It's time for you to give yourself a chance.

No, I can't. I already made someone to deal with my past trauma and turned him into a cold-hearted person and I don't want that to happen with Che. Che is the perfect one I ever met and I don't deserve him. He needs a peaceful life and I know I can't give him that. All I can do is let him go.

My girl, let's not talk about Che for now, Let's talk about you. Said Madhu.

There's nothing to talk about me. I screamed in tears to her.

There is. I have been telling you to go for psychology counseling, did you? Why can't you work on yourself rather than end up hurting others?

Madhu...Please. I shouted at her.

I'm sorry. She said and came to hug me but I pushed her back.

Look, I know I need to give myself a chance but at the same time, I can't cheat myself in the name of psychology counseling. I said.

How long will you cheat yourself by being against things that can help you?

Madhu, Please... I need a solution to face the reality, not to escape it. I said and she looked at me and didn't speak for a few seconds.

And that solution starts with you. Said Madhu and left the room. I fell asleep with all those tears rolling over my face. I know I'm in my self-sabotage phase and I don't want him to be a victim. Madhu says that I'm not ready to give myself a chance but I can't risk someone's life for giving myself a chance. From all those moments I spent with him, I learned that he deserves someone who can help him reach his dreams and protect him from all his fears, Someone who could make him happy, really happy, flying colors happiness but I'm unlucky since I can't be that someone he needs. People may wonder why I'm concerned this much for someone whom I haven't known even for a week but a few know that there's no time bound in love and all it takes is an honest moment we share and feel with him. These are the moments in my life when someone walks into our life who's the one for us but we cage ourselves for their happiness than us. The helplessness that comes with knowing we can't change what's happening, the ache of seeing the struggle, or the frustration of feeling like things are beyond our control, all of this can weigh heavily on the heart. It's in these times that our resilience is truly tested. The strength it takes to witness these moments and go through them is not small. It speaks to the courage that lies within me, the courage to face reality, no matter how hard it may be.

CHAPTER V

TUESDAY
16:01 HRS

Che.

Hey. He said.

Where are you? I asked him through a call.

Home.

Can we meet?

Yeah sure, I need to go to Pondicherry to check on a property, do you mind joining me?

When we will be back?

By tomorrow. Will meet the property owner by 10 in the morning and will leave by 12, also I have a flight at midnight. So will directly go to Chennai Airport from Pondicherry.

Flight?

Yeah, I need to go to Kuala Lumpur tomorrow.

Why? I asked him.

Yeah, A business proposal to present.

Seems like you are occupied fully, let's meet sometime later.

Nah, it's fine. Come let's go.

Huh?

Are you coming?

Yes.

Great, get ready, will pick you up in an hour. He said and I cut the call. I told myself that this would be my last trip with him and called Madhu.

Yes. She said and by her tone, I can understand that she is angry at me.

I'm leaving for Pondicherry with Che. I said.

Okay?

I'm going to tell him before we return to Chennai.

Tell him what? Asked Madhu.

That I'm leaving. I said.

Mandhakini, Please don't do anything stupid like this. I cut the call before she completed it. After an hour I heard someone ringing the bell and I sensed it should be Che and took my bag, opened the door, and saw Madhu.

Have you gone Mad or what? She shouted and came in.

Sorry, Am I at the right time? Asked Che from behind.

Che, You're here? I called him in.

Che, this is Madhu.

I do remember seeing her on that night. He said and gave his hands to Madhu. Later Madhu called me in for a minute but I refused.

It's okay, if you guys need some time, I'll wait outside. Said Che.

No, it's nothing. I rushed to the door and said to Che that we could start. He looked confused by seeing my behavior and looked at Madhu.

Yeah. he said and said bye to Madhu. The moment we got into the car, I became selfish and decided not to tell him. I just rested my head on his shoulder.

Feels like you're not okay. He said.

Nah, I'm fine. I said and smiled.

Hope you are. He said and, he played some tracks by AR Rahman and we sang together and traveled towards Pondicherry by seeing the Bay of Bengal in the ECR.

Are you Love? I asked him.

Maybe.

With?

Should I say?

No. I said and turned toward the ocean. I wish I could talk more with him but I know that doesn't make any sense hereafter at the same time I feel guilty by seeing the excitement he carries. The inner battle I go through is getting bigger every second. We reached the Pondy entrance and it was already 10 at night, I thought that we would go hit the hotel but he turned the car into the Auroville Beach. He got down and asked me to get down. He didn't say anything that night, he just took a cigarette and sat by facing Ocean. I felt he was not okay and walked towards him. I sat next to him.

Che, are you okay?

Yeah. He said and smiled back. That smile wasn't that good enough and I could sense the pain he was hiding behind his smile.

Do you mind talking it out?

Yes.

Yes. I said and there was a minute of silence prevailed.

This place saves a beautiful and sad love story.

Your past? If I'm not okay, that false sexual accusation?

Yes. I said and he smiled again.

The days when I lost hope in people started here. Few things cost your whole life to prove your innocence and one such incident is that. My happiness stays in making people happy but I expected that back from them and ended up getting a worse punishment for expecting it. Not alone the memories follow us, even a few places in those memories will haunt us. By the time he finished saying this, I witnessed his tears.

Then why did you come here?

To tell my scars that this place and memories can't haunt me anymore. He said and held my hand.

I turned towards him and kissed his lips. The moment I kissed him, I started feeling guilty for the things I was going to do for him but I became selfish that night. We sensed the droplet of water between our lips, the sky started pouring on us within seconds. We didn't mind it, instead, we held our faces and continued kissing.

Che, Do you love me? I asked him. He came forward and continued kissing me.

I Love You Mandhakini. He said. Thanking the rain for helping me to hide my tears. I moved to hug him. We were just hugging each other in the middle of the beach in the rain. Slowly we stood up and went to the car. Once we sat down inside the car, we were looking at each other, and suddenly his phone started ringing. He answered the call and started the car. We went inside our hotel room and he passed me the towel. He asked me to use the restroom and sat on the couch. I went to the restroom and stopped. I turned back.

Che, Make love to me.

Huh?

I wanna feel your love to the fullest.

I need a whole lifetime for it.

No, Show me. Now. I insisted. He held my hand and made me sit on his lap.

I wanna feel your touches. I said.

And?

All over me. Now.

And?

Proceed. I said. He passed through my skin with his lips. He slurped the droplets of rain all over me. He spreads all those droplets all over me in every dry place in my body. I passed his hands inside my brassiere and touched them like he owned them. He pressed my waist and looked at me.

I badly needed this, from you. These touches can't be defined as Lust, Right?

He nodded.

Che.

Mandhakini?

Own me. Completely. I said and lay out my legs towards him.

Please. I said. He touched my inner thighs and came forward towards my face.

I Love You. He said and I touched his face. My inner voice was saying that he's your last, even if he is not going to be in your life. He sensed the tears in my eyes.

What happened?

I'm happy. I said to him and he kissed my forehead and said I love you. He made me look at him and made me feel his phallus in me. All the sexual education on having proper sexual satisfaction flew away over the emotional satisfaction I had that night. We cuddled each other and went to sleep. I was struggling to sleep but I was happy to see him sleeping so peacefully. I didn't know when I fell asleep, but when I woke up, I saw him sitting right in front of me.

CHAPTER VI

Che?

Thank you.

Why?

It has been years since I had a peaceful sleep. Years since I fall asleep without those rolling tears. Thank you. He said. I was just staring at him.

Okay, you take a rest, I'll be back in an hour. He said and moved to the door.

Wait. I said.

I'll also come with you, hope you're not late for your meeting. I said and looked at my watch.

Okay, in that case, pack your things and come, let's head to Chennai post the meeting. He said. I got ready within 15 minutes and rushed to him. We then moved to his meeting with a property owner there and I was just looking at him with all the sorrows I carry. Later an hour, we started to head towards Chennai.

I've arranged a driver at Chennai Airport, he will drop you at your home. Sorry, I couldn't drop you on my own. He said.

No, it;s okay. I'll take the metro.

Anyhow you need to take an auto from Nandhanam Metro to your house, so...

It's okay, I'll manage.

Sure?

Yeah. I said and maintained silence back to Chennai. He was concerned about me after seeing my silence but I told him that I was tired.

So, I'll be back in 15 days. I'll miss you. He said.

Me too. I'll miss you.

It's already late, shall I?

Yeah, Oh wait. I stopped him.

Yeah?

Can I come in? Atleast until check-in?

Here, there's no visitor ticket option available, you can't. He said.

Oh, then... Bye. Take care.

Bye. He said and moved towards his terminal. Suddenly he turned back and came to me. He hugged me and kissed me on my forehead.

I Love You. He said and went inside the Airport. I moved from there to the metro station and purchased a ticket to Nandhanam Metro Station. I went and sat at the platform. I lost 7 trains by now since he left. He loved the way I wanted and I achieved it by being selfish, but in the long run, I can't be so. It is a selfish act to make him stay even after knowing that he deserves someone better. All the love I know is to let them go and I have to let him go now. With all the Battles, I came down in the rain and started crying in my lone den of unhappiness.

THURSDAY

01:25 HRS

Hey, I landed and just checked him. I received a text from him.

Take Rest Che. I texted back and hugged my tear-filled pillow. The next day when I woke up he sent me a room tour of his stay and shared all his excitement about being there in his private infinity pool and said that he is going to take me there with him the next time. He started including me in everything he came across and I brought some courage and texted him.

Che? Are you Free?

Yes.

I know, this will hurt you but I'm sorry. I have told you about my past relationship right? He's back and I've decided to give him another chance. Hope you understand. It was so beautiful with you but I can't. I'm sorry. Sorry. I texted him and the moment he saw the message, I blocked him on all the social media accounts and ended a beautiful one-werk story with a stranger turned lover.

CHAPTER VII

AFTER 20 DAYS

"Phone rings"
Madhu.
I met Che. She said from the other side.
Where?
At his Restobar.
What did he say? I asked him.
I went there with my friends. He saw me and came to talk. He took me to his office. He was looking so disappointed and depressed.
Where is she? He asked.
She's in Karnataka, Mysore.
By any chance, will you meet her?
Yeah, for her birthday.
Hmm... Can you pass a letter to her on behalf of me? He asked.
Sure. I said and he started penning down a letter for you. Later he sealed the letter and gave it to me. It was hard for me and I couldn't resist myself from saying this to him.
She lied. I said.
I know. Said Che.
What? You told him that I lied to him? Why Madhu? Why did you say so? I yelled at her.
Even if I didn't, he does know that you lied.
Where's the letter?

CHAPTER VIII

Mandhakini,

Nobody looks good in their darkest hours, even I wasn't until you came. Souls don't meet by accident, like how we met and gone through all emotions. There's no shortcut to forgetting someone. You just have to endure missing them every day like how I miss you every second. And I know it's not easy or possible to forget you. We would have heard that "it's not the person we miss, it's the memories that follow" but here more than memories it's the person. You're my permanent obsession and it's you who makes me smile and feel loved whenever I'm tired. Is 7 days this big? We passed weeks and weeks but that one week with you is life, love. The intimacy we share is the best in all the universe and the intimacy I speak of is not alone related to the sexual aspects. It's how we were and dreamed together and those dreams made us meet. I used to say settle for someone who gives you enough assurance for you to avoid overthinking. Find someone that boosts your self-confidence and won't let you feel insecure. Someone willing to comfort and understand you when you're struggling or don't have the energy to talk. We all deserve that someone, and that one "Someone" has always been you. I understand how much reassurance you need now, from my side I'm honestly here to live a life to prove you that. From manifesting a future with you, now you have become my manifestation for life. Rehabilitated hearts always deserve a chance and that chance for rehabilitating starts from us. There's always a door for starting things again from first. Please stay in my life until my heart stops beating.

I Love You

Che.

Che. I called him and he turned back.
Mandhakini?
I Love You.